# Baba Yaga
## The
## Flying Witch

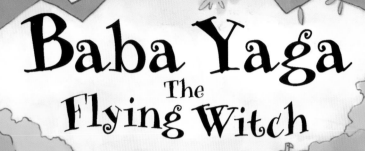

Retold by
Susanna Davidson

Illus...
Sa...

Reading Consultant: Alison Kelly
Roehampton University

F
DAV

This story is about
a witch called
Baba Yaga,

a little girl
called Tasha,

a magic
hut,

a dog,                          a cat

and a
magic doll.

3

Once upon a time, in a far off land, lived a little girl called Tasha.

Her mother died when she was very young.

But before she died, she gave her daughter a tiny doll.

"Give the doll food and water if you are ever in danger," she said. "She will help you."

6

A few years later, Tasha's father married again. "A new wife for me and a new mother for Tasha," he thought.

But his new wife had other ideas.

One morning, she waited
for Tasha's father to go to
market.

Then she called
for Tasha.

"While I'm out, I want you to go to Baba Yaga's hut in the forest."

Ask her for a needle and thread.

But Baba Yaga is a witch!

Tasha sat on the doorstep
and took her doll from her
pocket.

She gave her a little piece of
bread and a sip of water.

The little doll ate. The little doll drank. Then her eyes lit up like stars.

"Take some bread for Baba Yaga's dog," said the doll.

"And some ham for Baba Yaga's cat. Do not fear. I will protect you."

13

Tasha packed the ham
and bread. Then she set out
through the deep, dark forest.

Soon, a wild wind began
to blow.

The trees creaked.
Their branches groaned.
Tasha looked up...

...and saw Baba Yaga
zooming through the
forest in a flying pot.

15

She pushed herself along
with a wooden spoon.

And wiped away her tracks
with a long, wooden broom.

Tasha followed her to a strange little hut. It twirled around on chicken's legs...

...and winked at Tasha with its window-like eyes.

Baba Yaga stood in front of her hut and sang.

"Magic hut, magic hut, turn around,
Bend your legs and touch the ground."

The magic hut spun around
on its bony legs and replied,

"I can dance, I can see
A little girl, in front of me."

"A-ha!" said Baba Yaga.
"What have we here?"

"P-p-please," said Tasha.
"My stepmother sent me for
a needle and thread."

20

Baba Yaga smiled a dreadful smile. Her mouth was full of iron teeth.

Her hair was greasy. Her hands were warty. Her nose reached down to her chin.

"I can help you," croaked
Baba Yaga. "But first you
must sweep my hut."

Baba Yaga called for her maid. "Make me a nice big fire," she said.

"I'm going to eat that little girl for lunch!"

Inside the hut, Tasha began
to sob. "I don't want to be
eaten," she cried.

24

"Then give me that ham," said a skinny, black cat, "and I'll help you."

"Now, run away as fast as you can," purred the cat.

But first, take these.

"Baba Yaga will chase you. When you hear her coming, throw down this mirror."

26

"If she keeps on coming, throw down this comb."

Tasha took the mirror and the comb and ran outside...

...where Baba Yaga's big, black dog was waiting.

It snarled. It growled.
It showed its sharp teeth...

...and Tasha threw it
the bread.

"Keep running!" barked
the dog. "Keep running!"

Back came Baba Yaga. "Are you sweeping, little girl?"

"Yesssss, I'm sweeping," hissed the cat.

Baba Yaga leaped into her hut. "Where's the girl?" she screamed at her cat.

"I've served you for a long time," said the cat. "But you've never given me food."

31

Baba Yaga raced out
to her dog.

"Why didn't you stop her?"
she shouted.

"I've served you for a long time," said the dog. "But you've never given me food."

"That girl gave me bread to eat."

33

Baba Yaga didn't wait a moment longer. She jumped into her pot.

She pushed off with her wooden spoon.

And she flew off,
sweeping away her tracks
with her long, wooden broom.

**Thump! thump! thump!** went the spoon. Swish! swish! **swish!** went the broom.

"Baba Yaga's coming," cried the little doll.

Tasha threw down
the mirror.

It became a wide,
wide river.

"Curses!" cried Baba Yaga.
She bent her bony body and
drank and drank and drank.

Soon, there wasn't a drop
of water left.

Then once again, Tasha heard the **thumping** spoon and the **swishing** broom.

"Baba Yaga's coming," cried the little doll. Tasha threw down the comb.

40

A huge mountain sprang
up behind her.

"Curses!" cried Baba
Yaga. She began to chew
through the mountain.

But her iron teeth were rusty from drinking the wide, wide river.

One by one, her iron teeth snapped.

"Curses!" cried Baba Yaga. "I can't fly over the mountain. I'll have to go back."

With a **thump! thump! thump!** and a **swish! swish!** swish! Baba Yaga sped back to her magic hut.

Tasha didn't stop running
until she reached home.

Her father rushed out to
meet her. "Where have you
been?" he asked.

"Stepmother sent me to Baba Yaga's hut," said Tasha. "And the witch tried to eat me."

"Then it's time your stepmother left," said her father.

And he threw her out of
the house.

She was never seen again.

Series editor: Lesley Sims
Designed by Maria Pearson
Digital manipulation by Louise Flutter

First published in 2008 by Usborne Publishing Ltd., Usborne House,
83-85 Saffron Hill, London EC1N 8RT, England. www.usborne.com
Copyright © 2008 Usborne Publishing Ltd.